For Julian

Did you know?
The following groups of animals are called...

A **Memory** of Elephants

A **Parliament** of Owls

A **Convocation** of Eagles

A **Pride** of Lions

An **Obstinacy** of Buffaloes

A **Bask** of Crocodiles

A **Dazzle** of Zebras

A **Bloat** of Hippopotami

A **Cackle** of Hyenas

A **Tower** of Giraffes

A **Crash** of Rhinoceros

A **Confusion** of Wildebeest

A **Troop** of baboons

A **Leap** of Leopards

A **Collision** of Cheetahs

A **Business** of Mongeese

A **Flamboyant** of Flamingoes

A **Mop/Gang/Clan** of Meerkats

See if you can spot them in our story!!!

he air on the hot African horizon, floated in wavety waves...

One dry day, Bella the Elephant, who lived in an enormous National Park called The Savannah, looked up at the bright sky and took a deep breath. The air was sweet and heavy with the scent of the Gerbera Daises that littered the plains and she paused to look at their beautiful red, pink and white colours.

Nearby, a butterfly fluttered lazily in the air. Bella saw it and then playfully gave chase, before she finally gave up and decided instead to have a roll around in a patch of tall grass.

Her parents kept a protective eye over her and her siblings and all the while, the herd of elephants, or memory, as it is also known, moved slowly through the grass and picked fruit from the Marula trees, munching on them as they went.

Bella followed along and occasionally peeked through the leaves, observing anything that helped to satisfy her curiosity.

On Bella's trunk sat Julian, the Chameleon.
Julian was Bella's best friend and he was
enjoying a free ride whilst he basked in the sun.
His skin had turned the same colour as Bella's
and if it wasn't for the fact that Bella was
talking to him about the warm sunny day,
you wouldn't have known he was
there.

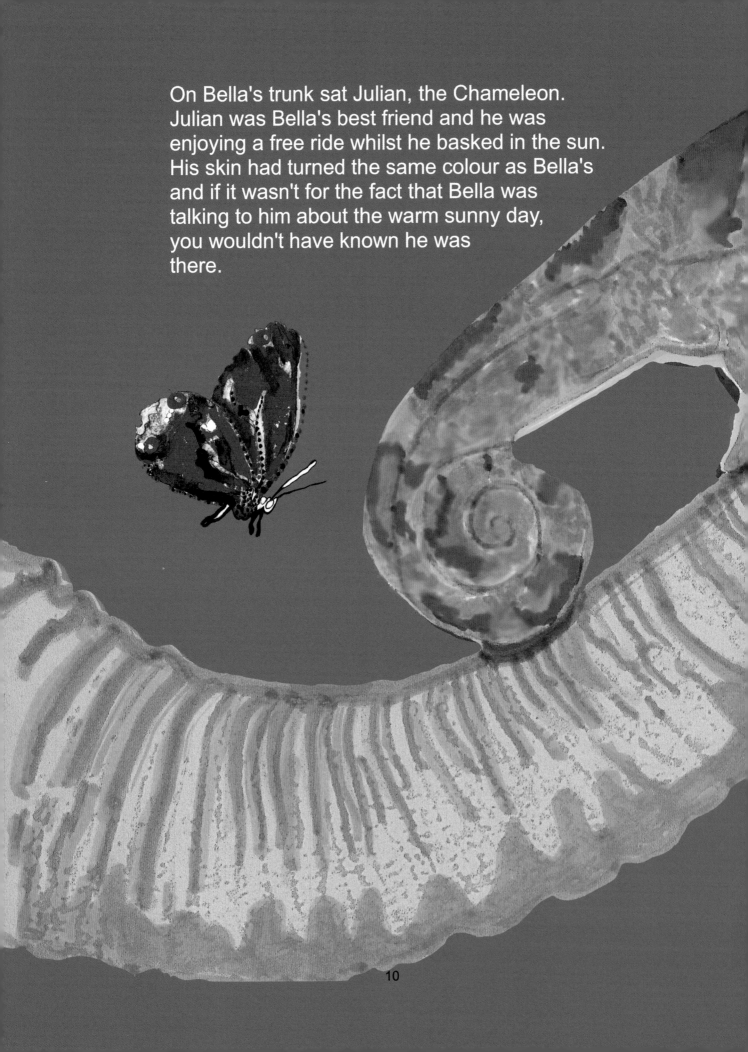

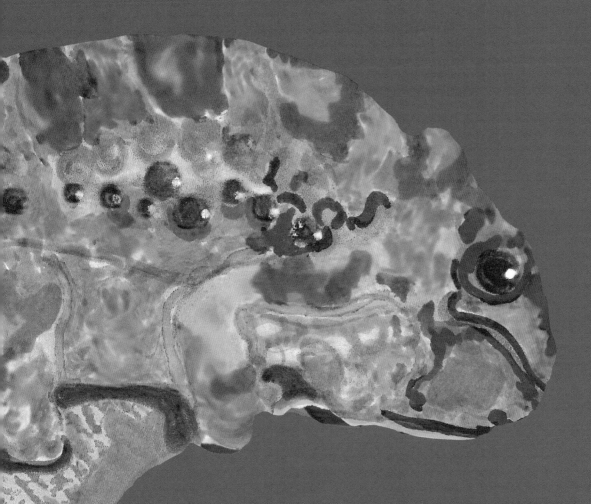

He moved slowly towards a fly that was wandering along
the edge of Bella's trunk for although he knew he wasn't the
fastest animal on the plain, he did have a sticky tongue that he
could use, with lightning speed.

This, along with an ability to swirl his eyes independently of each
other, which gave him superior vision and his wizard-like ability to
match any surrounding colour in a flash, help him to keep himself fed
and safe.

Bella noticed that behind some bushes, the air was buzzing with
excitement. Somewhere, something was happening.

Suddenly she heard a noise.

Clickety **click**, clickety **click**.

"**What was that?**" Bella asked.

In the distance, she spotted Zelda the Zelebrity Zebra, whose silhouette was outlined by the bright flashes of dozens of cameras.

Clickety Click , Clickety Click.

Mesmerised by her beauty, crowds of admirers had gathered around her in their cars and were taking photos.

Zelda stood proudly with her head held high in the air. Her black and white striped skin shimmered in the sunlight.

Bella stood and watched, hypnotised by the beautiful pattern and thought to herself.

"Is that black with white stripes, or white with black stripes..."

clickety click
clickety click

In an instant, Bella felt jealous. She looked down at her own reflection in a small pool of muddy water.

"Why do I look so different? I'm the colour of stone! My trunk is so big and my feet are so large. Even my ears! They're so wide!" she said, angrily.

"Well, that's the way you were born, Bella," said Julian.

Bella looked back towards Zelda.

"She's the star! She's the most striking animal on the plains...and she KNOWS it!

How I would love to look like her... Walk like her... Talk like her and BE like her," she whimpered.

"You don't need to, Bella," whispered Julian.

Bella shot him a stern look.

"Oh, what do YOU know? YOU can be whoever you want to be. You can change your skin colour into any colour you want, without even thinking! I'm stuck like this FOREVER!!!"

"I want to be admired too. I want to be a tourist attraction and to have everyone take MY picture!"

Just then, a wonderfully clever idea entered Bella's head.

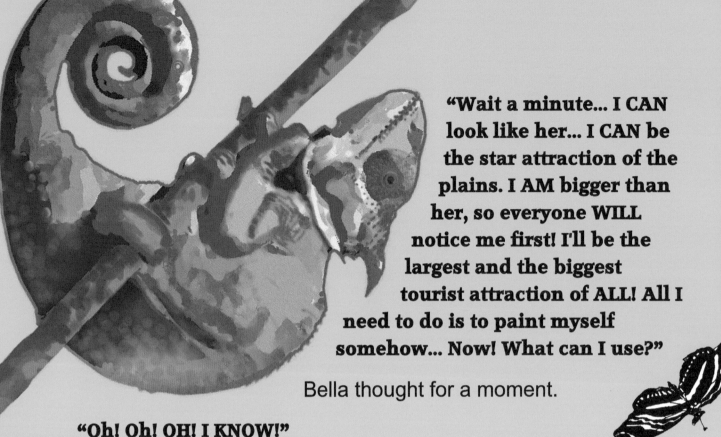

"Wait a minute... I CAN look like her... I CAN be the star attraction of the plains. I AM bigger than her, so everyone WILL notice me first! I'll be the largest and the biggest tourist attraction of ALL! All I need to do is to paint myself somehow... Now! What can I use?"

Bella thought for a moment.

"Oh! Oh! OH! I KNOW!"

She remembered a patch of natural asphalt that was close by.

"ELEPHANTABULOUS!!!" she exclaimed. **"That would be perfect!"**

"I don't think this is a good idea, Bella..." whispered Julian, concerned.

"Oh SHOOSHOOWEEBA!" shouted Bella, cutting him off mid sentence.

She ran to an almost dry riverbed, where natural asphalt was seeping through the cracks in the ground.

Julian curled his tail around a long branch that was hanging down from a nearby Marula tree and lifted himself into the leaves. From there, hidden and out of sight, he kept one eye on Bella and used the other to keep a lookout for any signs of danger.

"That is Pik, Julian. Look! That would be perfect!"

Bella dipped her trunk into the thick black, chewy substance and let it drip into her gaping mouth.

"Yum, yum YUM!!! It has a twisted taste of Liquorice!!!"

Using her trunk as a paintbrush and using the pitch black pik as paint, Bella started to paint her body with large black stripes.

Splashety Splash! Splashety Splash!

She admired her reflection in the water and was extremely pleased with the result. She complimented herself for having such a brilliant idea.

"OH I look JUST like Zelda! Only BIGGER, BOLDER and BRIGHTER! Now EVERYONE will see me!"

"Bella, be careful..." warned Julian.

"Oh, SHOOSHOOWEEBA Julian," she snorted.

Bella walked off through the open veld to show off her new look.

She raised her trunk high into the air and made a loud trumpeting sound which attracted everyone's attention...

Everyone...including Abigail...the Lioness!

Abigail lowered herself into the tall grass.

"Well hello! Why haven't I noticed this extraordinarily large Zebra before?" She thought to herself. **"Look at those HUGE Stripety Stripes!!!"**

She moved forward, slowly.

"Well! What can one say? This MUST be my lucky day!"

In the animal kingdom, it is normally the majestic Lioness that does all of the hunting, whilst the male lions remain stretched out underneath the trees and bask lazily in the sun.

Abigail snaked through the tall grass without a sound, her body colour blending in perfectly with those of her surroundings.

In an instant, Zelda's friends caught Abigail's scent on the air.

"Something is wrong!" they cried. **"We know that smell. It's a...LION!!!"**

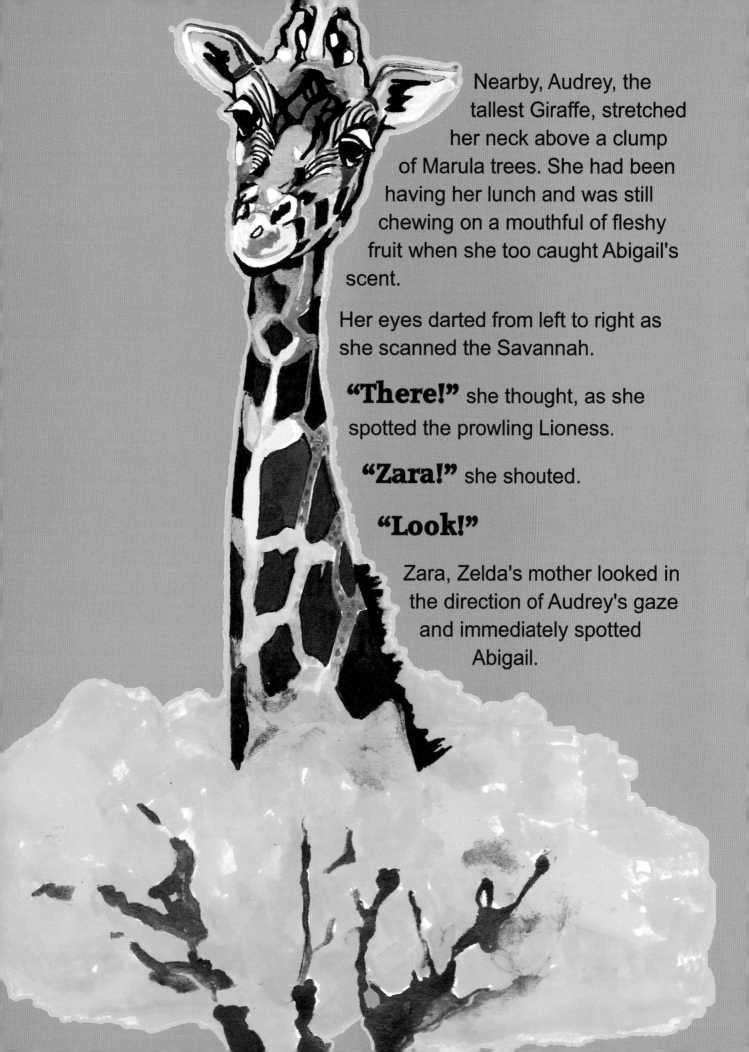

Nearby, Audrey, the tallest Giraffe, stretched her neck above a clump of Marula trees. She had been having her lunch and was still chewing on a mouthful of fleshy fruit when she too caught Abigail's scent.

Her eyes darted from left to right as she scanned the Savannah.

"There!" she thought, as she spotted the prowling Lioness.

"Zara!" she shouted.

"Look!"

Zara, Zelda's mother looked in the direction of Audrey's gaze and immediately spotted Abigail.

In a **flash** and a **dash**, the Dazzle of Zebras moved as one. They rushed to Bella and circled around her, to blur Abigail's vision with their striped skins. They knew that her sight was not as good during the day as it was at night and this was meant to confuse her.

Irritated and angry, Abigail leapt from the grass with a great **ROAR!** She crashed down onto an empty space where she thought Bella should have been, before tumbling over onto her back in a dusty cloud.

"Where are you?" she shouted.

Abigail sneezed loudly and squinted, but all she could see was a huge wave of black and white that shimmered and moved in the dust. She felt dizzy and slowly turned around and made her way back into the grass to lie down and sulk.

From there, she watched, defeated as the Zebra moved towards the waterhole, cheering.

"One day!" she thought. **"One day, WILL be my lucky day!"**

Zelda, looked at Bella sternly.

"Why have you tried to copy my skin?" she asked.

Bella noticed that the stripes on Zelda's head almost resembled a frown and was immediately embarrassed.

She swung her trunk over her back.

"I've always wanted to look like you," Bella stammered.

"You're so beautiful. Everyone wants to take your picture. You're the star of the reserve and everyone comes to see you. But I don't have your skin, so I thought I'd paint mine to look like yours and then everyone would notice me too."

"Mmm, that's true," said Zelda. **"You WILL be noticed...as**

LUNCH!"

"I mean... Look at what's just happened? Your vanity could have caused the demise of not only you, but that of your friends and family too! What were you thinking?"

Bella looked down at her feet.

"I just wanted to be beautiful," she whispered, faintly.

Bella's mother moved towards her. She reached out her trunk and gently rubbed Bella's back, before wiping away a tear that rolled down Bella's cheek.

"You are an amazing, majestic elephant, Bella. Your colour and size acts as your greatest protection. It's our differences that protect us in the wild," she said, reassuringly.

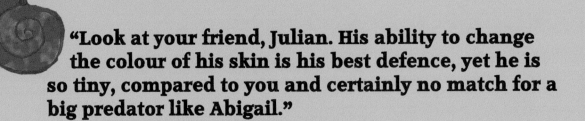

"Look at your friend, Julian. His ability to change the colour of his skin is his best defence, yet he is so tiny, compared to you and certainly no match for a big predator like Abigail."

Bella hung her head in shame.

"We are both proud animals, complimenting each other and all together, the soul of Africa. We adorn the great landscape and we all attract admirers since we are all unique," explained Zelda.

"But it's the Elephant that is part of the biggest tourist attraction of the Savannah. The world famous Big Five that everyone talks so much about and that everyone rushes in from all corners of the planet to see. The Elephant...NOT the Zebra. Did you know that?" said Zelda.

"She's right, you know," said Bella's mother. "We are indeed part of the Big Five. The Pride of Lions. The Crash of Rhino. The Leap of Leopards. The Gang of Buffalo and finally us. The Memory of Elephants. We form a unique group of animals and together, we are only found here in Africa. It's our home. Even the Lions belong here and have their own place."

Bella lifted her head and smiled, shyly.

"So, do you really think the animals find me beautiful?"

"Of course!" exclaimed Zelda.

"Your OWN beauty is very powerful and if you toss it away, you throw away your own power! You are the guardian and the keeper of this land. All of the animals look up to you. You are beautiful just the way you are and everyone knows it..."

Zelda took a great sigh.

"...and so do I!"

Bella looked at her new found friend and was filled with joy. She would never have believed that Zelda and the others thought so highly of her.

The Elephants and the Giraffes surrounded her and slowly splashed her with water until the sticky stripes were washed away and she was clean again.

Bella was so happy that she jumped straight into a muddy puddle and rolled around, whilst blowing loudly from her trunk.

Everyone laughed.

"Welcome back, you magnificent little elephant!"

And for the first time ever, Bella was grateful to just be herself.

An Elephant!

WHO told the story?...We did!!! WHY?? Because we LOVE telling stories!!! WHO painted the pictures and designed the book?

Annette & Lindi DID!!! WHY? ... Because it's FUN!!!

Printed in Great Britain
by Amazon